THE RED BALLOON

ALBERT LAMORISSE

THE RED
BALLOON

A **Doubleday** Book for Young Readers

Photographs in this book were taken during the filming of the movie THE RED BALLOON
Screenplay, direction and photographs, A. Lamorisse · Chief cameraman, Edmond Sechan
Cameraman and photographer, P. Goupil · Music by M. le Roux · Sound, E.Vuillemin · Editing,
P. Gillette · Production manager, M. Pezin · Assistant directors, E. Agabra and A. Fontaine
Production secretary, L. Haas · Script-girl R. Bource

Published by Delacorte Press, a division of
Bantam Doubleday Dell Publishing Group, Inc.,
1540 Broadway, New York, New York 10036.

Doubleday and the portrayal of an anchor with a dolphin
are trademarks of Bantam Doubleday Dell Publishing Group, Inc.

LE BALLON ROUGE
© A. Lamorisse, 1956
All translation, reproduction and adaptation rights reserved
ISBN: 0-385-00343-9 Trade

ISBN: 0-385-14297-8 Paperback

LIBRARY OF CONGRESS CATALOG CARD NUMBER 57-9229

30 29 28 27 26

Once upon a time in Paris there lived a little boy whose name was Pascal. He had no brothers or sisters, and he was very sad and lonely at home.

Once he brought home a lost cat, and some time later a stray puppy. But his mother said animals brought dirt into the house, and so Pascal was soon alone again in his mother's clean well-kept rooms.

Then one day, on his way to school, he caught sight of a fine red balloon, tied to a street lamp. Pascal laid his school bag on the ground. He climbed up the lamppost, untied the balloon, and ran off with it to the bus stop

But the conductor knew the rules. "No dogs," he said. "No large packages, no balloons."

People with dogs walk.

People with packages take taxis.

People with balloons leave them behind.

Pascal did not want to leave his balloon behind, so the conductor rang the signal bell and the bus went on without him.

Pascal's school was a long way off, and when he finally reached the school door it was already shut. To be late for school and with a balloon—that was unheard of! Pascal was very worried.

Then he had an idea. He left his balloon with the janitor, who was sweeping the yard. And since it was the first time that he had ever been late, he was not punished.

When school was over, the janitor, who had kept the balloon in his room for Pascal, gave it back to him.
But it had begun to rain. And Pascal had to walk home because of those silly rules about balloons on buses. But he thought his balloon shouldn't get wet.

There was an old gentleman just going by, and Pascal asked him whether he and the balloon could take shelter under his umbrella. So, from one umbrella to another, Pascal made his way home.

His mother was glad to see him finally come home. But since she had been very worried, she was angry when she found out that it was a balloon that had made Pascal late. She took the balloon, opened the window, and threw it out.

Now, usually when you let a balloon go, it flies away. But Pascal's balloon stayed outside the window, and the two of them looked at each other through the glass. Pascal was surprised that his balloon hadn't flown away, but not really as surprised as all that. Friends will do all kinds of things for you. If the friend happens to be a balloon, it doesn't fly away. So Pascal opened his window quietly, took his balloon back inside, and hid it in his room.

The next day, before he left for school, Pascal opened the window to let his balloon out and told it to come to him when he called.
Then he picked up his school bag, kissed his mother good-by, and went downstairs.
When he reached the street he called: "Balloon! Balloon!" and the balloon came flying down to him.
Then it began to follow Pascal—without being led by a string, just as if it were a dog following its master.

But, like a dog, it didn't always do as it was told. When Pascal tried to catch it to cross the street, the balloon flew beyond his reach.

Pascal decided to pretend he didn't care. He walked up the street just as if the balloon weren't there at all and hid behind the corner of a house. The balloon got worried and hurried to catch up with him.

When they got to the bus stop, Pascal said to the balloon: "Now, balloon, you follow me. Don't lose sight of the bus!"

That was how the strangest sight came to be seen in a Paris street— a balloon flying along behind a bus.

When they reached Pascal's school, the balloon again tried not to let itself be caught. But the bell was already ringing and the door was just about to close, so Pascal had to hurry in alone. He was very worried.
But the balloon flew over the school wall and got in line behind the children. The teacher was very surprised to see this strange new pupil, and when the balloon tried to follow them into the classroom, the children made so much noise that the principal came along to see what was happening.

The principal tried to catch the balloon to put it out the door. But he couldn't.
So he took Pascal by the hand and marched him out of school. The balloon left
the classroom and followed them.

The principal had urgent business at the Town Hall, and he didn't know what to
do with Pascal and his balloon. So he locked the boy up inside his office. The
balloon, he said to himself, would stay outside the door.

But that wasn't the balloon's idea at all. When it saw that the principal had put
the key in his pocket, it sailed along behind him as he walked down the street.

All the people knew the principal very well, and when they saw him walking
past followed by a balloon they shook their heads and said: "The principal's
playing a joke. It isn't right; a principal should be dignified, he shouldn't be
playing like one of the boys in his school."

The poor man tried very hard to catch the balloon, but he couldn't, so there was
nothing for him to do but put up with it. Outside the Town Hall the balloon
stopped. It waited for him in the street, and when the principal went back to
school the balloon was still behind him.

The principal was only too glad to let Pascal out of his office, and to be rid of
him and his balloon.

On the way home Pascal stopped to look at a picture in a sidewalk exhibit. It showed a little girl with a hoop. Pascal thought how nice it would be to have a friend like that little girl.

But just at that moment he met a real little girl, looking just like the one in the picture. She was wearing a pretty white dress, and she held in her hand the string . . . to a blue balloon!

Pascal wanted to be sure she noticed that his balloon was a magic one. But his balloon wouldn't be caught, and the little girl began to laugh.

Pascal was angry. "What's the use of having a trained balloon if it won't do what you want?" he said to himself. At that very moment some of the tough boys of the neighborhood came by. They tried to catch the balloon as it trailed along behind Pascal. But the balloon saw the danger. It flew to Pascal at once. He caught it and began to run, but more boys came to corner him from the other side.

So Pascal let go of his balloon, which immediately rose high into the sky. While the boys were all looking up, Pascal ran between them to the top of the steps. From there he called his balloon, which came to him at once—to the great surprise of the boys in the gang.

So Pascal and his balloon got home without being caught.

The next day was Sunday. Before he left for church, Pascal told his balloon to stay quietly at home, not to break anything, and especially not to go out.

But the balloon did exactly as it pleased. Pascal and his mother were hardly seated in church when the balloon appeared and hung quietly in the air behind them.

Now, a church is no place for a balloon. Everyone was looking at it and no one was paying attention to the service. Pascal had to leave in a hurry, followed out by the church guard. His balloon certainly had no sense of what was proper. Pascal had plenty of worries!

All this worry had made him hungry. And as he still had his coin for the collection plate, he went into a bakeshop for some cake. Before he went inside he said to the balloon: "Now be good and wait for me. Don't go away."

The balloon was good, and only went as far as the corner of the shop to warm itself in the sun. But that was already too far. For the gang of boys who had tried to catch it the day before saw it, and they thought that this was the moment to try again. Without being seen they crept up to it, jumped on it and carried it away.

When Pascal came out of the bakeshop, there was no balloon! He ran in every direction, looking up at the sky. The balloon had disobeyed him again! It had gone off by itself! And although he called at the top of his voice, the balloon did not come back.

The gang had tied the balloon to a strong string, and they were trying to teach it tricks. "We could show this magic balloon in a circus," one of them said. He shook a stick at the balloon. "Come here or I'll burst you," he shouted.

As luck would have it, Pascal saw the balloon over the top of a wall, desper-
ately dragging at the end of its heavy string. He called to it.
As soon as it heard his voice, the balloon flew toward him. Pascal quickly
untied the string and ran off with his balloon as fast as he could run.

The boys raced after them. They made so much noise that everyone in the neighborhood stopped to watch the chase. It seemed as if Pascal had stolen the boys' balloon. Pascal thought: "I'll hide in the crowd." But a red balloon can be seen anywhere, even in a crowd.
Pascal ran through narrow alleys, trying to lose the gang of boys.

At one point the boys didn't know whether Pascal had turned right or left, so they split up into several groups. For a minute Pascal thought he had escaped them, and he looked around for a place to rest. But as he rounded a corner he bumped right into one of the gang. He ran back the way he had come, but there were more boys there. He was desperate—he ran up a side street which led to an empty lot. He thought he'd be safe there.

But suddenly boys appeared from every direction, and Pascal was surrounded.

So he let go of his balloon. But this time, instead of chasing the balloon, the gang attacked Pascal. The balloon flew a little way off, but when it saw Pascal fighting it came back. The boys began throwing stones at the balloon.

"Fly away, balloon! Fly away!" Pascal cried. But the balloon would not leave its friend.

Then one of the stones hit the balloon, and it burst.

While Pascal was crying over his dead balloon, the strangest thing happened! Everywhere balloons could be seen flying up into the air and forming a line high into the sky.

It was the revolt of all captive balloons!

And all the balloons of Paris came down to Pascal, dancing around him, twisting their strings into one strong one and lifting him up into the sky. And that was how Pascal took a wonderful trip all around the world.